FUSION

DECONSTRUCTED / DIETS

SPLIT UP A
SANDWICH

by Shalini Vallepur

BEARPORT
PUBLISHING

Minneapolis, Minnesota

Library of Congress Cataloging-in-Publication Data is available at www.loc.gov or upon request from the publisher.

ISBN: 978-1-64747-526-0 (hardcover)
ISBN: 978-1-64747-533-8 (paperback)
ISBN: 978-1-64747-540-6 (ebook)

© 2021 Booklife Publishing

This edition is published by arrangement with Booklife Publishing.

For more information, write to Bearport Publishing, 5357 Penn Avenue South, Minneapolis, MN 55419. Printed in the United States of America.

PHOTO CREDITS

All images are courtesy of Shutterstock.com, unless otherwise specified. With thanks to Getty Images, Thinkstock Photo, and iStockphoto. Front Cover - VWORLD, PILart, Tortuga, AKaiser. Recurring Images - VWORLD, mything, AKaiser, PILart. 4-5 - Africa Studio, ArtAdi, Gruffi, margouillat photo, VectorShow. 6-7 - Frame Art, Kach233, Hugh Manatee. 8-9 - photominer, SGr, VelP,. 10-11 - Alfmaler, Antonio Gravante, Bogdan Wankowicz, Frolova_Elena, Ildi Papp, mything, Oqvector, pirtuss. 12-13 - Elena Shashkina, HandmadePictures, Maquiladora, Nickola_Che, vandycan. 14-15 - Africa Studio, Martial Red, Ngukiaw, Tim UR, Anna.zabella, mamormo. 16-17 - etorres, Magicleaf, mything, Reamolko, Vasilyeva Larisa, Elegant Solution, Ansty. 18-19 - D. Pimborough, koss13, winterstorm. 20-21 - DorotaM, ducu59us, JRP Studio, sarsmis, YuliiaHolovchenko. 22-23 - Nuttocook, telse, THANAPHON SUBSANG.

CONTENTS

WHAT IS A DIET?

Your diet is what you eat and drink in a day. The foods we eat help us to grow and be healthy.

Our meals are made from lots of different **ingredients**. It can be hard to know exactly what is in our food or where it comes from.

Lots of different ingredients go into spaghetti and meatballs.

Let's look at all the ingredients in a sandwich!

SERVING SANDWICHES

Sandwich-like foods have been eaten for a long time. *Rou jia mo* is a dish of meat between bread. This dish has been eaten for thousands of years in China.

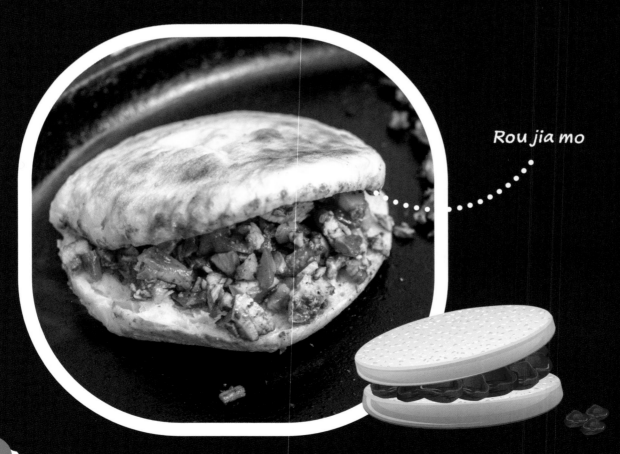

Rou jia mo

Sandwiches as we know them today were first eaten in England in 1762. John Montagu, the **earl** of a place called Sandwich, ate meat between **slices** of bread.

Bring me some meat bread!

JOHN MONTAGU

John loved sandwiches because they can be eaten with one hand.

SPLIT UP A SANDWICH

Sandwiches can have different ingredients. This sandwich is called a BLT.

Bread

The BLT gets its name because it is made of bacon, lettuce, and tomato.

Mayonnaise

Bacon

Tomato

Meat, fish, and eggs can all be put in sandwiches.

Lettuce

Spreads, such as peanut butter and jelly, are also tasty sandwich fillings.

Let's learn about each ingredient.

DID YOU KNOW?

Around 300 million sandwiches are eaten in the U.S. every day!

BREAD

Bread is a very important part of a sandwich.

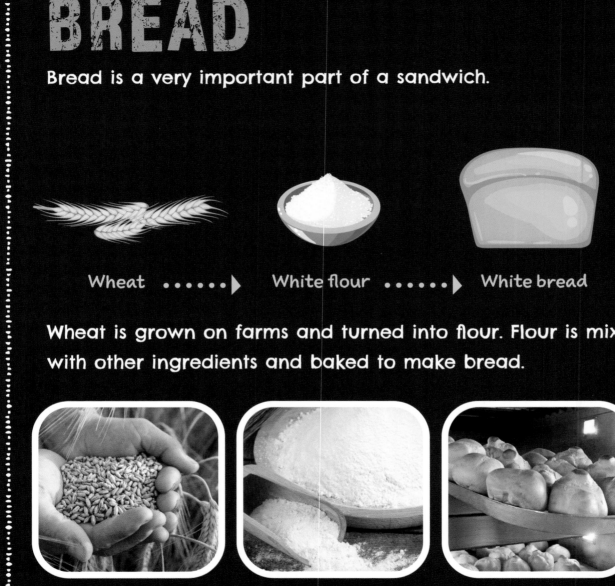

Wheat ......▶ White flour ......▶ White bread

Wheat is grown on farms and turned into flour. Flour is mixed with other ingredients and baked to make bread.

When wheat is turned into white flour, some of the **nutrients** are lost. Wheat bread is made from wheat flour, which has more nutrients in it.

Wheat

Wheat flour

Wheat bread

Wheat bread contains more **fiber** than white bread. Fiber is good for us.

Wheat bread

MEAT

Some sandwiches have meat. Bacon can go into sandwiches.

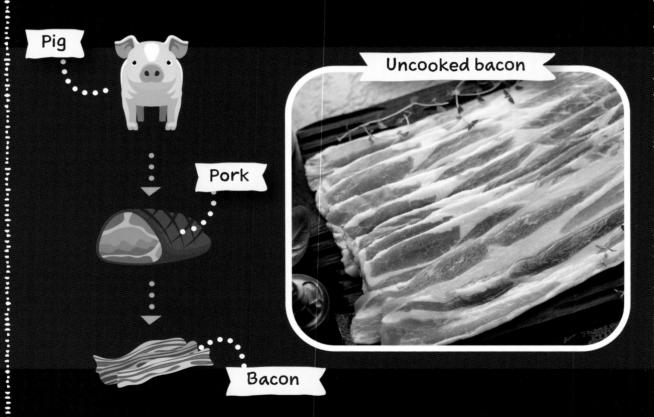

Pig

Pork

Bacon

Uncooked bacon

Bacon often comes from pigs. It needs to be cooked before it is safe to eat.

Eating lots of bacon can be unhealthy. This is because it has other ingredients, such as salt, added to it.

Cooked bacon

Salt

Too much salt is not good for our bodies.

VEGGIES AND FRUITS

Sandwiches can have lots of toppings. Many people put fruits and vegetables on their sandwiches.

Lettuce leaves

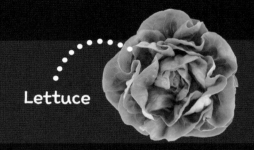

Lettuce

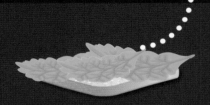

Lettuce leaves give sandwiches a fresh crunch.

Sliced tomato

Tomato

Tomatoes can be sliced and put on sandwiches.

Lettuce and tomato are always in a BLT sandwich. They contain nutrients that we need to grow and stay healthy.

Add fruits and veggies to any sandwich!

SAUCES

Sauces give extra flavor to a sandwich.

Tomatoes are mixed with other ingredients to make ketchup.

Mustard seeds are mixed with other ingredients to make this sauce.

Vinegar + Egg yolks + Oil = Mayonnaise

Mayonnaise, or mayo, is used in lots of sandwiches.

Have you had any of these sauces on a sandwich?

Many sauces are made from healthy ingredients. However, if they have too much sugar or salt, they are not as good for us.

Hummus can be used like a sauce. It is made from chickpeas.

SMART SWAPS

Sandwiches can be made with lots of different ingredients. They can be made to fit lots of different diets.

There are many ways to eat sandwiches.

Sandwiches don't need to have meat. Cheese sandwiches can be eaten in a **vegetarian** diet.

Cheese sandwiches can be toasted to melt the cheese.

Sauce

Try cheese with sauce.

SUITABLE FOR VEGETARIANS

A person following a **vegan** diet does not eat anything from animals, such as meat, cheese, or eggs.

Tofu

Tofu is a tasty topping that is not meat.

Vegan meat looks and tastes like meat but does not come from animals.

VEGAN FRIENDLY

Using bread without wheat makes sandwiches safe for people who can't eat **gluten**.

Gluten-free bread

SANDWICHES AROUND THE WORLD

People enjoy many tasty sandwiches.

Sandos are eaten in Japan. Sandos can use meat or fruit.

Pork sando

Fruit sando with cream

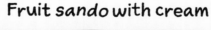

Sandwiches can be made from different types and shapes of bread.

Banh mi is a type of sandwich from Vietnam that is made using baguettes.

GLOSSARY

earl	someone who is royal from the United Kingdom in Europe
fiber	a part of some foods that takes longer for the human body to break down
gluten	a part of wheat that makes dough sticky
ingredients	the different foods that are used to make something
nutrients	natural things that humans need to grow and stay healthy
slices	thin pieces of food that are cut, or sliced, from something large
vegan	a diet in which people do not eat things from animals, such as meat, cheese, or eggs
vegetarian	a diet in which people do not eat meat or fish but still eat dairy and eggs

INDEX